"To Dayle, for teaching me it is never *the end*."

There once lived a BEAUTIFUL princess...

and could paint
a picture that looked

like REAL LIFE.

She loved reading books,

and was an EXCELLENT dancer.

But most importantly

she was dating a very handsome PRINCE.

who played the bass and also had long, flowing hair.

She thought her life was absolutely Perfect.

Until one night...

her prince decided that he didn't want to be her prince any more.

She was very sad.

She cried for a very long time.

The only thing that made her happy was knitting.

So she knit,
 and purled,
  and yarned over,

until she had a scarf that was over twenty feet long!

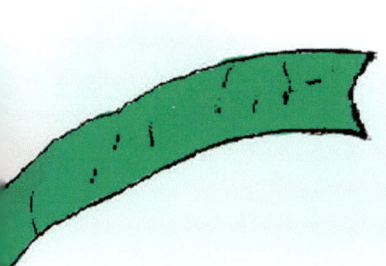

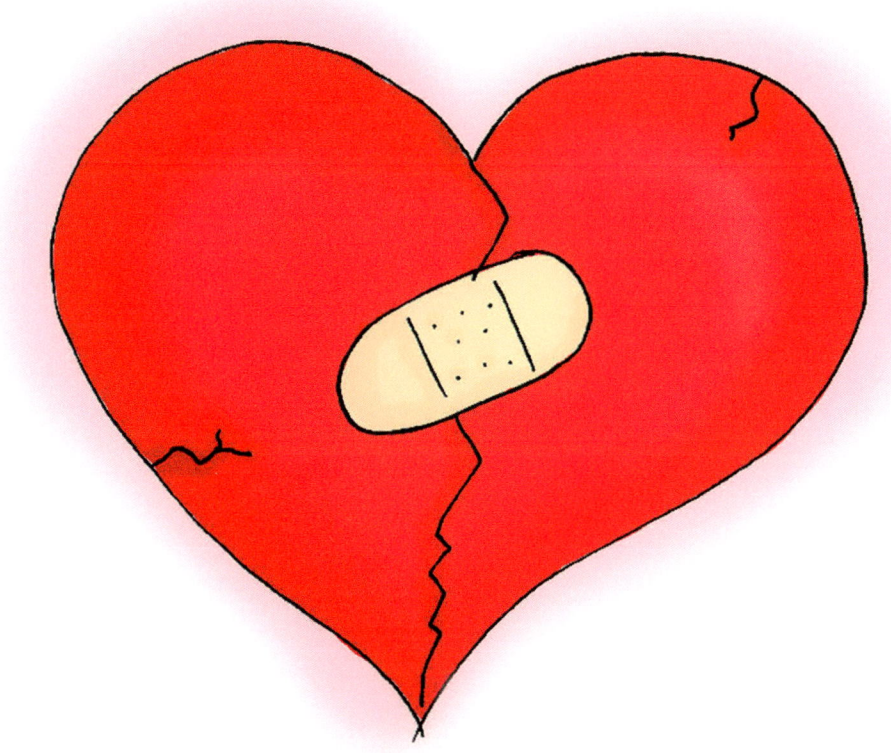

she decided that
she ought to start living her life.

She did yoga.

And painted.

And hung out with her friends.

She realized she had a **loving** mother.

And wrote a whole bunch of angry letters that she never sent.

Although she may have kissed a few frogs along the way.

Eventually she forgave the prince,

and she was happy with who she was.

Also she bought 30 cats.

The Beginning...

Copyright © 2014 by Richelle Burchill

First Edition – April 2014

ISBN
978-1-4602-3715-1 (Paperback)
978-1-4602-3716-8 (eBook)

All rights reserved.

No part of this publication may be reproduced in any form, or by any means, electronic or mechanical, including photocopying, recording, or any information browsing, storage, or retrieval system, without permission in writing from the publisher.

Produced by:

FriesenPress
Suite 300 – 852 Fort Street
Victoria, BC, Canada V8W 1H8

www.friesenpress.com

Distributed to the trade by The Ingram Book Company

Richelle Burchill

learned early that the first step to getting what you want is imagining yourself on the path to receiving it. She loves to work hard, and enjoys reading, dance and drawing. She hopes to inspire young people with her books.

CPSIA information can be obtained
at www.ICGtesting.com
Printed in the USA
LVIC06n1255300414
383748LV00001B/1